J.M. BRUM • ILLUSTRATED BY JAN BAJTLIK

OUR CAR

A Neal Porter Book

ROARING BROOK PRESS

New York

Our **car** is as red as a fire engine.

My **dad's** legs are so long he gets into the car without opening the doors.

The **wind**
tickles us as we ride.

When it starts to
rain we put up the
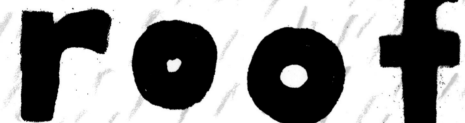

In the winter, when we have lot of snow, Dad puts on special **tires.**

In the summer, we take our **trailer** with us.

When the **gas** runs out, we have to push the car.

Sometimes the **engine** screeches like a wild animal.

Then the

mechanic

has to take a look...

We **wash** the car when it gets dirty.

At night its

headlights

show us the way.

Today

get to drive.

But **Mama** says:

"Just don't park on the rug!"